For Ernesto
D.C.

For Magali
S.M.

Little Pea
Text copyright © 2016 Davide Cali
Illustration copyright © 2016 Sébastien Mourrain
First edition copyright © 2016 Comme des géants

Editorial and art direction by Nadine Robert
Translation by Nick Frost
Book design by Jolin Masson

The illustrations in this book were made with ink and digitally colored.
This book was typeset in Louize.

This edition published in 2023 by Milky Way Picture Books,
an imprint of Comme des géants inc. Varennes, Quebec, Canada.

Library and Archives Canada cataloguing in publication

Title: Little Pea / Davide Cali; illustrations, Sébastien Mourrain.
Other titles: Petit Pois.
English.Names: Calì, Davide, 1972–author. | Mourrain, Sébastien, 1976–illustrator
Description: Translation of: Petit Pois.
Identifiers: Canadiana 20220010242 | ISBN 9781990252112 (hardcover)
Classification: LCC PZ7.1.C35 Li 2022 | DDC j843/.92—dc23

ISBN: 978-1-990252-11-2

Printed and bound in China

Milky Way Picture Books
38 Sainte-Anne Street
Varennes, Qc J3X 1R5
Canada

www.milkywaypicturebooks.com

story by
Davide Cali

art by
Sébastien Mourrain

Little
Pea

Milky Way
Picture Books

When Little Pea was born,
he was little. Very little.

So little that his mom made
his clothes specially by hand.

So little that he had to borrow
shoes from his dolls.

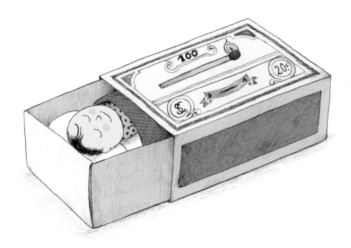

So little that he could fall asleep

in the unlikeliest of places.

At an early age,
he taught himself how to swim.

As he got older, he wrestled bears,

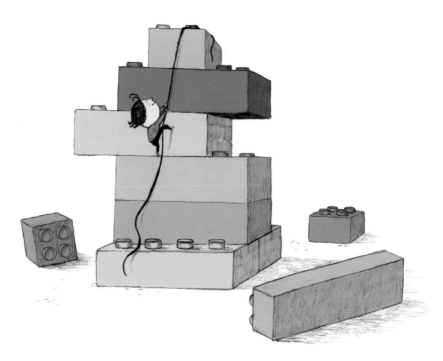

scaled new heights,

walked tightropes,

and raced his own car.

In summer, he liked to venture into the garden

for a stroll

and a dip in the pond.

Sometimes, he laid under the stars
and imagined how big the universe was.

He also loved to read,

climb tomato plants,

and go
horseback
riding...

sort of.

When Little Pea started school,
he quickly realized how little he actually was.

Too little for his chair,

too little to play the recorder,

too little for gym class,

and too little for his lunch.

At recess,
Little Pea couldn't play with the other kids
for fear of getting squished by a ball
or stepped on by a classmate.

So he began drawing pictures
to cheer himself up.

Still, his teachers worried about him.
"What will become of poor Little Pea?"

But loneliness never
kept him down. Years later,
Little Pea grew up... a little.

Today, he has a lovely
home that he built himself.
And he grows his own tomatoes.

Every day,
he hops in his car and drives to work.

At his tiny office,
everything is just the right size.

What does Little Pea
do for a living, you ask?
Take a guess!

He draws stamps that people use
to send letters in the mail!

Turns out, you're never
too little to be a big artist.